# THE CHAMPIONS

## FRANCES MACKAY

Ransom

On the Ball
**The Champions**
by Frances Mackay

Published by Ransom Publishing Ltd.
Radley House, 8 St. Cross Road, Winchester, Hampshire SO23 9HX, UK
**www.ransom.co.uk**

ISBN     978 178127 702 7
First published in 2014

Illustrated by Doreen Lang at GCI

ON THE BALL

# THE CHAMPIONS

## FRANCES MACKAY

The sixth book in the series
*ON THE BALL*

Matt was moving into Ben's house.

'Your mum's so great to let me stay here,' said Matt.

'Well, we couldn't let some other school have our best player, could we?' said Ben.

'Come on, leave that 'til later – let's go to the park.'

Later that week, Mr Jones called a meeting.

'Well done, team, for winning against Brent Park. What a match, eh? I am very proud of you all,' said Mr Jones.

Ben looked at Matt and smiled.

'This week, we play Green Street Junior. They're a strong side and they also won their first match – so we're in for a good game.'

'I've made a few changes to the line-up this week," said Mr Jones, and he wrote the team on the board.

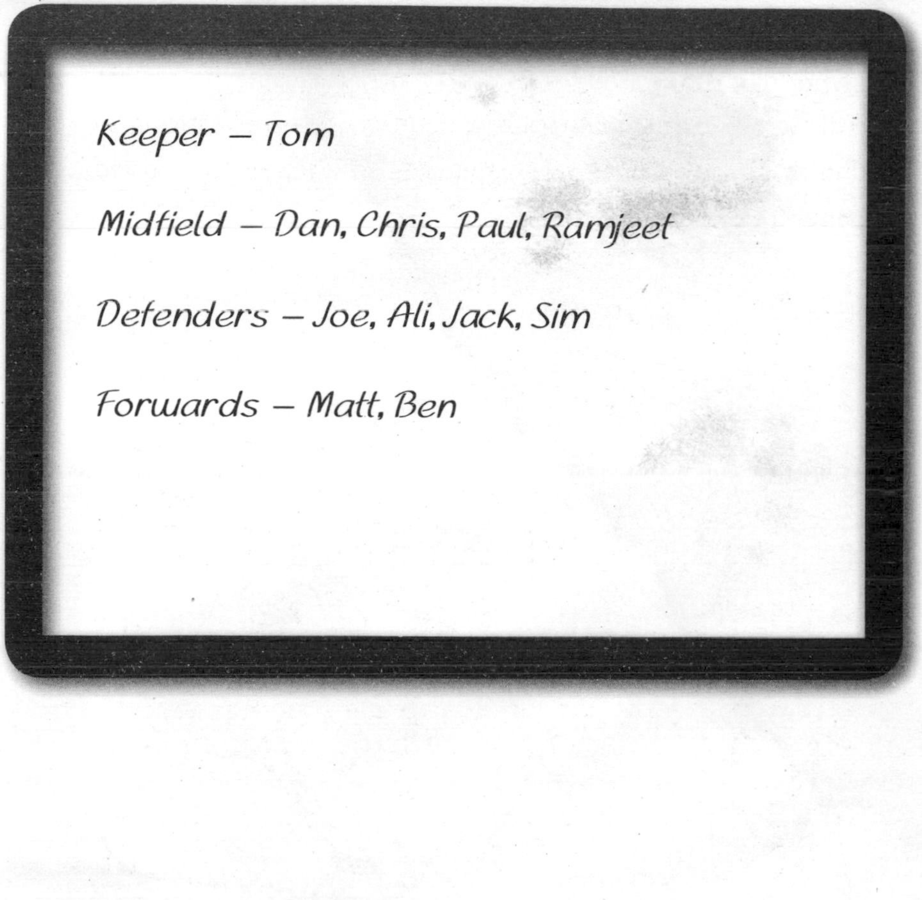

Keeper — Tom

Midfield — Dan, Chris, Paul, Ramjeet

Defenders — Joe, Ali, Jack, Sim

Forwards — Matt, Ben

'David's ankle is still not right, so he'll be out this week. Ramjeet did very well last week, and I want to give Ali a go, so the subs will be Oliver and Sara,' said Mr Jones.

'Keep up your practising and we'll be in with a chance.'

'What about our strip? Any news?' asked Dan.

'Sorry, no. You'll have to play in your PE kits again, I'm afraid,' said Mr Jones.

It wasn't what the team wanted to hear.

8

Saturday soon came round.

Ben and Matt were up early.

They both felt really excited.

'Can't wait for this match. It was great last week. I'm sure we can do it again,' said Ben.

'Yeah,' said Matt. 'But I still wish we had a team strip.'

'Me too,' said Ben.

The boys went downstairs.

'Are you ready to take us, Mum?' Ben asked.

'Sorry love, I'm afraid I can't take you today,' she said.

'Oh? Aren't you coming to the game?' asked Ben.

'Um … I've got something to do first. Dan's dad is picking you up. I'll try and make it later,' she said and she rushed out the door.

'That's strange. I wonder what she's up to,' thought Ben, as they went out.

Ben, Matt and Dan arrived at the game just as David was getting out of his dad's car.

He limped over to them.

'Knock 'em dead!' he said.

'We will,' said Ben.

'Just make sure you're ready for next week. We need you on the team,' said Matt.

In the changing room everyone was putting on their PE kits.

'I hope Green Street don't laugh at us like Brent Park did,' said Dan.

'Yeah, so do I,' said Ben.

'OK team. Listen up,' said Mr Jones. 'Green Street will be tough to beat — but I'm sure we can do it. Just remember what we practised at training and you can't go wrong. All ready? Then line up.'

'Wait!' shouted a voice, as some people came rushing in.

It was Ben's mum with Mr Baker, the manager of the supermarket.

'Mum! What are you doing here?' asked Ben.

'Well ... I have a big surprise,' she beamed.

'I told Mr Baker how your football strip had been stolen, and he was very keen to do something about it. He knew how hard you had all worked to raise the money for the strip. So ... he has bought you a new one. Look!'

Mr Baker held up one of the shirts.

It had the school's name on the right and the name of the supermarket across the front.

Everyone's eyes lit up. They couldn't believe they finally had their strip.

'Oh, wow!' said Ben. 'Mum, you're the greatest!'

'Yeah – and thanks, Mr Baker, this is brilliant!' said Matt.

'Well, what are you waiting for? Don't just stand there – put it on!' laughed Mr Jones.

Everyone quickly put the strip on.

Soon the whole team was standing in line in their brand new strip.

No one could say they weren't a proper team now.

Green Street won the toss and kicked off, but this week Ben's team was on the attack right from the start.

Matt scored a goal in the first five minutes.

'Brilliant goal, Matt!' said Ben.

From then on it was end-to-end play, until a lack of marking let Green Street fire home the equaliser on the stroke of half-time.

'OK team, listen up,' said Mr Jones.

'That was a very good first half. Sim, Ali, you've done some solid defending, and Tom, you made some excellent saves. Keep it up, and remember, just do your best.'

In the second half, Ben's team had two shots at goal that just went over or went wide.

But then Dan tucked home the rebound from a shot from Paul and they were 2-1 up.

'Yes!' shouted Dan, as he fell to his knees in front of the goal.

'We're on a winner now, guys, keep it up,' said Matt.

Joe was subbed off and Oliver came on.

Sim and Ali defended really well. Green Street were unable to get their strikers within reach until just before the end of play, when they were given a corner.

Everyone seemed to hold their breath as the Green Street striker lined himself up.

Ben looked worried.

The striker stood still for a while, then took aim and fired.

The ball slammed home.

2-2.

'Sorry, guys,' said Tom.

'It was a good try, Tom. Come on, we can still do it,' said Matt.

But it was not to be.

Tom pulled off a spectacular save, but Ben's team didn't score again.

The whistle blew and it was still 2-2.

'What a fantastic match,' said Mr Jones later. 'Green Street's the team to beat and you put up a good fight. Well done everyone!'

'I felt more like I was part of a real team in our new strip, but we still didn't win,' said Ben.

'No – but they didn't win either,' laughed Matt.

Six weeks later, they were to meet Green Street again — in the finals.

Ben's team had played some excellent matches.

They were much better players now — so they were ready for the big final.

'Well, this is it. We finally made it!' said Matt.

'Yeah, I can't wait to beat the socks off Green Street,' said Ben.

There were lots of supporters on the side-lines.

It looked like everyone at school had come to watch.

Sam had made a big red banner – with all the team's names on it.

There were lots of supporters for Green Street, too.

Ben had never played in front of so many people.

He had butterflies in his tummy as they walked out on to the pitch.

'Go for it, Ben!' yelled Ben's mum.

This made him smile.

Ben waved back.

'Yeah – go for it,' yelled Sam, and everyone from school cheered.

Ben's team won the toss and kicked off.

Dan made an excellent pass to Matt, who was well placed for goal, but a good tackle by a Green Street defender gave them the ball.

Green Street quickly scored with a header from a fine cross.

Ben's team picked up the pace and equalised with a neat goal by Dan, after a goal-mouth scrabble.

But Green Street were on top in the first half and had two more chances at goal.

Tom made some excellent saves, and it was still 1-1 when the whistle blew.

Mr Jones called the team together.

'A great start. Our defence is letting us down, though – so keep it tighter, Sim. Excellent saves, Tom, you're doing really well. Keep the pace up everyone. This is it, now – good luck!' said Mr Jones.

The second half started with a lot of midfield play.

Both teams were playing really well, but after twenty minutes neither side had scored.

The supporters tried to boost the team.

'You can do it!' yelled Sam.

'Come on, Ben,' yelled Ben's mum.

'I want my strip holding that cup!' yelled Mr Baker.

Ben's team pulled themselves together.

They wanted to win so much – they just *had* to do it.

In the last ten minutes, Dan and Chris dominated the midfield, keeping Green Street in their own half.

With only three minutes to go, Matt finally got his chance.

He positioned himself well and scored a fantastic goal from outside the box, after a superb through ball from Ben.

'Yes!' yelled Matt, as he punched the air.

The supporters went wild!

Sam was jumping up and down, shouting his head off.

'Yaaaay ... Matt!' he screamed.

It was to be the only goal of the second half.

Green Street tried hard to regain the ball, but it wasn't their day.

The whistle blew and Ben's team were the champions!

For a moment, Ben just couldn't believe it.

He stood very still, watching everyone go wild around him.

Then Matt rushed over, almost knocking him to the ground.

'We did it! We did it!' he yelled.

'Yeah mate – we did it!' Ben yelled back.

The team was presented with a trophy.

Matt held it up and everyone cheered.

The Daily Press interviewed Mr Jones.

They took a team photo.

Ben couldn't stop smiling.

He was so happy he thought he might burst.

All the hard training had been worth it.

He was a champion!

Later that week, Ben's mum showed him the newspaper report about their big day.

'I'm so proud of you, Ben,' said his mum, giving him a hug.

'From always being last, you're now first! I knew you could do it.'

# THE DAILY PRESS

## SCHOOL WINS CHAMPIONSHIP

### Local School Wins Trophy

On Saturday our local school won the school's league football championship defeating Green Street Junior by one goal.

There was a huge crowd of supporters for both sides and

they were not disappointed by the excellent play on both sides.

## Football Strip Thief Caught

A man has confessed to stealing and destroying the brand new football strip from our local primary school.

He admitted to the theft after he was caught breaking into the school earlier today.

The man was behaving strangely and kept yelling out "Revenge! I did it for Revenge!"

# HOW MANY HAVE YOU READ?

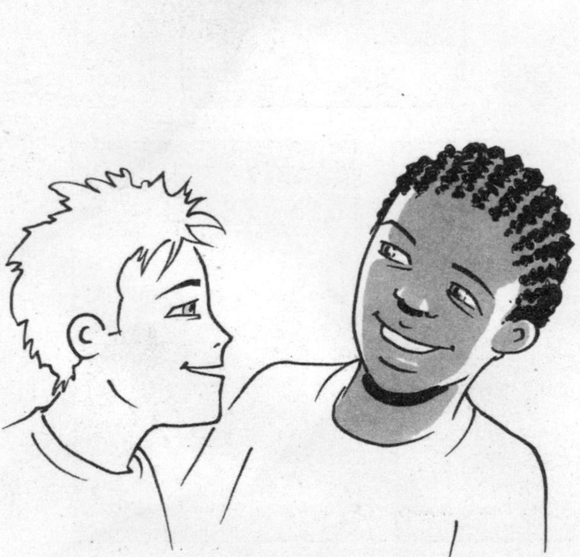